The Fart Book 2

Diary of a Stinky Kid

J.B. O'Neil

J. J. Fast Publishing, LLC
7760 E State Route 69, C5-330
Prescott Valley, AZ 86314
(757) 6JJ-FAST

ISBN: 978-1973794493

Table of Contents

FREE BONUS – Fart Book 2 Audiobook

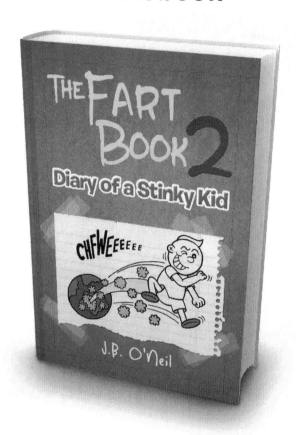

Hey gang...If you'd like to listen to the hilarious audiobook version of "Fart Book 2: Diary of a Stinky Kid" while you follow along with this book, you can download it for free for a limited time by going here:

www.funnyfarts.net/fartbook2

My Stinky Story

Hi, My name is Milo Snotrocket and I just moved to Flatulata Flats, Wyoming. It's been a little hard adjusting to my new lifestyle here, and one of the biggest things I've had trouble with is making friends. At my old school, I was the best farter in the entire 4th grade. I personally thought I was the best in the entire state! My ability to pass gas made it a breeze when it came to making friends.

Everyone wanted to know the guy who could voluntarily emit such a wide variety of booms and boms. Here, it's not so easy. People see me as just an ordinary kid, and they have no clue that they are in the presence of a fart genius.

My mom tells me to be patient, that these average people will discover my talent one day, but I don't have time to wait. I'm tired of sitting with the nerds at lunchtime. I want to stand out and get the recognition I deserve. Now is the time for me to begin farting my way to victory.

A Close Call

Step one in my journey to fart-empowered friendship and fame in my new school was to act like the cool kids. I tried dressing like them, talking like them, and even walking like them, and nothing worked. All of my attempts to be cool had the opposite effect, because now everyone thought I was an uncool wannabe. My final attempted idea was to eat like them, and boy, was that interesting.

At Flatula Flats Elementary School, you had options when it came to lunch. You could get the Chef's Surprise meal, or you could buy something from the Snack Shack, which sold chips, fruit snacks, and the holy grail of all things delicious-nachos. Tommy Tooty, the coolest kid in school, ate nachos from the Snack Shack every single day. The nachos weren't the best I had ever had but I was willing to make some sacrifices if it meant I would gain some friends from it.

So I ate my school bus yellow cheese nachos and headed off to science class, feeling a faint rumbling in my tummy. The storm had begun to brew inside of me, and there was no telling what could happen in the next hour filled with photosynthesis and life cycles. I set down my notebook and began to take notes of what was on the whiteboard, feeling more and more uncomfortable by the second. My stomach felt like a roller coaster, twisting and turning, heading straight for the exit, if you know what I mean.

My focus drifted from science to the thunderstorm inside of me. It began to roar and rumble, and by this point, the people around me could hear what was going on. I could feel the fart forming, and this was gonna be a good one. So good, I didn't even know what was going to come out. This could be my greatest opportunity to show the school my astounding ability, or it could be the end of my social career, before it had even begun. Sweat dripping down my forehead, I slowly raised my hand to ask Mrs. Lickabow to go to the bathroom, trembling more and more with the energy it took to hold my hand up high. After receiving permission, I bolted out the door, barely grabbing the bathroom pass on the way out. Half-running, half hobbling to keep the storm inside of me, I got to the bathroom, sat on the toilet, and let it all rip.

PFFFTHHHHHHHFTTTHHHTFHHHHTTFFHHHHHHP.   What   a
relief! The fart lasted a good minute and a half, and it
renewed my confidence in my special gift. I knew now that I
was ready to show Flatula Flats who the real Milo Snotrocket
was.

The Boomerang Bubbles

Gym class was my very first class of the day, and my least favorite subject. Our teacher had just given birth, so most of our curriculum consisted of postpartum exercises and sports. We were in our yoga unit when I experienced my very first Boomerang Bubble. I will admit, listening to Zen-sational nature sounds first thing in the morning helped me ease into the day nicely. However, two yogurt-squeezies and a cheesy breakfast burrito come back to haunt you when you are in downward dog.

We moved from yoga stance to yoga stance, each one challenging in its own way, because only the girls who took ballet class could actually perform the moves correctly. All the rest of us struggled with everything, except downward dog. This was my favorite yoga pose because all I had to do was touch the ground. It was relaxing and a nice break from all the acrobatic contortionist positions that were impossible to recreate. This morning, however, I got a little too relaxed.

Maybe it was the lack of sleep or just the soothing sounds entering my ears, but I lost my usual control over my body. I didn't even have to try or push anything out, because my body took over and let loose my first Boomerang Bubble. This fart crept up on me, and was alarmingly silent, except it didn't stay out. It came RIGHT BACK IN. Like a powerful gassy boomerang. It was tiny, but still left a slight aroma of bean and cheese breakfast burrito for all to enjoy. I smiled with delight as our teacher demonstrated the next pose-Wind Releasing Pose.

Chair Farts

Some of my favorite farts to release are chair farts, the kind where you roar from the rear and it stays on the chair long enough for you to sniff it back again. It's like a satisfactory comforting feeling that gives me the warm and fuzzies inside. I long to do these when I'm at school, because it only works on my favorite video game playing chair at home.

The fabric upholstery seems to grab the scent and keep it longer than ordinary wooden or plastic chairs. However, my class has library day on Wednesdays and if you're lucky enough to grab one of the four available cushioned chairs to read in, then you're in for a sweet, stinky time.

I had my eyes on one of those chairs for weeks, and finally got to sit in one of the soft seats last Wednesday. I quickly grabbed a random book and got cozy. Luckily, I had eaten lunch recently, and the chili dog I ate was just beginning to settle in.

A few people noticed how much I was smiling while reading "Bolivian History 1823-1855", but I wasn't even comprehending any of the words, because I was too busy dropping spicy bombs into the cushions. Like a seasoned chef, I knew just the right amount of spice and wind to concoct a masterpiece in my chair.

I even "dropped" my pencil on the floor a few times so I could stoop down and secretly catch a whiff of my sinus-clearing creation. My eyes watered slightly, a mixture of happiness and horror, but I blamed it on the emotional hardships the Bolivians experienced in the book. The few whiffs I took left me wanting for more to satisfy my nostrils.

Stress Farts

I don't know about you, but when there's a big test coming up (History class especially!) I get really nervous. So nervous, that I get the stress farts. They're the definition of tiny but mighty. Stress makes my farts go dead silent and smell like 14 day old rotten eggs. The worst thing about them is that they just keep coming out at a steady, fast rate. I can't even begin to think about controlling them because then I lose focus on what's more important-the test. I just have to let the toxic vapors flow out of my behind and not let it get in the way of my thoughts. In fact, sometimes they actually help me.

Last week, we had a fifty-two question exam on the Civil War and boy, was I nervous for that one. It was like I had an automatic gun with unlimited ammunition attached below my hips. I couldn't stop farting, but once I stopped trying to make them slow down and just let the fumes waft in the air around me, it was strangely comforting.

Even the people sitting nearby noticed the smell and content smiles slowly crept up onto their faces. I continued on with my test, feeling like I was drifting off into my own world. My own stinky, slightly rancid world.

Before I knew it, I had finished the test, and I was the first person in my entire class of twenty-six to be finished. In disbelief, I scanned my answers once again to make sure I had them all correct, and then turned the test in to my teacher with a big, satisfied smile on my face. When we got our grades back, I was slightly scared that I had totally flunked, but it turned out to be an A plus!

Not only that, but some of the kids that sat next to me gave me high fives and thanked me for helping them focus and get a good grade on the test too! Even Tommy Tooty, the coolest guy in school, invited me to sit next to him at lunch with all of his friends. I was finally starting to feel like I belonged, all thanks to my uncontrollable stress farts.

The Squeaky-Clean Squawk

Even though we only do boring yoga in gym class at this point, my mom says I stink a lot when I come home from school. I actually kinda like the way I smell nowadays, and sometimes I try to see how long I can go without washing my body. But my mom ("Party-Pooper Pat") has been making me take showers (not even baths!!!) almost every single day this week! I don't like it, but all this showering has definitely helped me discover some interesting fart facts.

Last Tuesday, after a hot, 45 minute long shower, I let loose an absolutely perfect fart. Judging by sound alone, it was the most idealistic, melodious, slightly wet, sputter to ever leave my body. It was the kind of fart that businesses would want to record to play back on soundboards and even movies and TV shows.

It was a squeaky-clean noise, and evidently came from my freshly bathed bottom. I even did two or three more to make my ears happy again, and make sure that that one beautiful fart wasn't just a fluke. It wasn't! The few that followed were just as wonderful as the first, and even the farts I let out after the other showers I took later that week sounded the same way.

Not only do shower farts sound great, but they also have a delightful stink to them as well. You'd think that my green apple scented body wash would mask any other "unpleasant" odors in the air, but you are wrong. Maybe it's knowing that my very own fart is the first of many contaminants to hit the fresh and fruity bathroom air that makes it smell so pleasing, or maybe it's simply just a scientific fact that shower farts will always smell like the best bad apples. Either way, knowing that I can depend on after-shower farts to be perfect every single time makes my heart sing a sweet song when they pop out.

Piano Lesson Farts

My mom signed me up for piano lessons recently. Definitely NOT my idea, but she tells me I can't play Super Sonic Boom (my favorite video game) unless I go once a week. So I do, obviously. While my friends at school think I'm cool and funny when I fart for them, my wrinkly old piano teacher doesn't appreciate my atomic toots as much as they do.

If I let any tiny little amount of gas pass while he is standing over my shoulder teaching me Middle C, he flips out and makes me APOLOGIZE and say EXCUSE ME, and to make things worse, he even clothespins his nose so he can't smell the sweet stench! It's terrible, and definitely physically hard for me to keep it all in for that forty-five minute time period when I'm supposed to be learning something that might have a slight impact on my future.

After so many failed attempts to hold back the gas, Mr. Tootzart threatened to stop teaching me, and my mom was not happy about that. I had one more chance to prove myself, or that was it. So, after school I tried everything to make sure that even if something slipped out, I'd be protected.

I put one of my little sister's diapers on, and even stuffed it with cotton balls to absorb any scent or sound. Sounds embarrassing, but luckily nobody except Tootzart and my mom would see me. When it was time to go, I threw on my baggiest pair of sweats to make it look normal, and it sort of did.

I farted a couple of times to see if my under-thunder diaper worked, and it did! I jumped into the car, and Mom and I drove off to piano lessons. It lasted the whole forty-five minutes and then some, and I played piano worry-free, thanks to my amazing invention.

The "Come Back to Me"

I am constantly passing gas, as you probably already know. Every minute of my life, something seems to just pop out, whether it's a good fart or not. Because there are so many, I've learned to sort of ignore the less important ones and focus on the gas of greater importance (like the big booms and the toxic thuds). However, sometimes a seemingly unimportant flutter of flatulence will escape, and I then catch a whiff of it later on, when the secretly intense fumes almost knock me off me feet. In a good way, of course.

Last night, my family and I had a pretty big meal of pork chops and mashed potatoes. It was actually one of my favorite meals I had eaten in a long time. I was enjoying my food so much, that even my bottom was silent and content. It stayed quiet the whole dinner, and only let one go as I got up from my seat to fill up my cup of Sizzly Spray.

I thought nothing of it because it was so light and airy, that it couldn't have possibly smelled like anything. It was so perfectly dainty and I am one hundred percent sure that's how princesses toot (it's impossible for princesses not to fart). I ignored that regal rip and filled up my cup, but when I came back to my seat I almost spilled my soda. Pheeeeewww-eeee! It was bad. So bad, but also so good.

Not only was it smelly enough to make me lose my appetite, but it had lingered in the air long enough for me to come back to it and actually take in the stench. I could have so easily missed it, and I wouldn't have even known what I had missed, but that didn't happen. The Regal Rip had turned into the Super Squeamish Stink Bomb, and after that, I paid just a little bit more attention to all of my tiny airy poots that followed.

Dutch Oven Farts

When buying Christmas presents for my mom the other day, I came across something I had never heard of before; a Dutch oven. I knew what an oven was, and I think I know where the Dutch live, but the two words sounded totally weird and foreign to me. I asked my dad what it was and he told me it was like a big, heavy pot made for stewing foods like sauces and soups, so all the flavors and scents get super strong and tasteful. I thought this sounded like the perfect name for my favorite before-bed activity.

The other night, after my parents had already turned off the lights, and I was just about to go to sleep, I did a good ol' Dutch oven fart (or at least that's my new name for them). My dad had tucked my new, fluffy comforter underneath my mattress so I knew there was no way for anything to escape without coming out of the top opening. My warm, insulated cover was sealed down onto my bed-just how I like it.

Now, the only farts that can ever go into a good Dutch oven are the ones that are so hot, that they burn on their way out, and smell of the Super Cheezy Burger Bonanza meal you ate at lunch earlier that day.

Because of this, Dutch oven farts are almost a rarity, and they can't happen every night. Tonight I had the perfect recipe in my brand-spankin' new high-end Dutch oven pot. I shimmied down a little lower into my bed and let the hot air shoot out, and double-checked to see if there were any places the steam could escape (there weren't).

The key to getting the full Dutch oven experience however, is not just the gas itself, but the fumatic aroma of the Super Cheezy Burger Bonanaza hitting your nose afterward. I quickly pulled the covers over my head so I was in a little Dutch oven tent and breathed in as much air as I possibly could, and before I knew it, I had fallen fast asleep.

Clothing Rack Farts

My absolute least favorite thing on this entire planet is shopping with my mom. She tells me "Oh, I'm just grabbing a few things, I know exactly where everything is". But then, she spends like 5 hours in there, just dragging me along behind her. I have no clue why she even wants me there, because I try very hard to be really annoying, in hopes that this is the last time I have to shop for women's pajamas ever again in my life.

However, she doesn't seem to mind, so I have to think of other ways to deal with this situation. Finding new ways to perfect the art of the fart is one of my favorite pastimes, as you already know. So naturally, I found a way to do this while my mom buys new clothes for everybody in her life.

While out shopping the other day, I came up with the most brilliant game that allowed to be my true gassy self and have fun while shopping. We were in the women's pajamas section so I definitely had to make my own fun in there and look really uninterested. I got comfortable near a round rack of pajama pants with my back to the clothes and let it rip. This allowed the clothes behind me soak up the smell like a sponge.

I did the same on the other side of the rack to even out the smell, and then continued to fart on all of the round racks in the area. It was like a pajama minefield! The absolute best part was watching the reactions on all of the old ladies' faces when they went to go take a look at some nice pajamas and immediately put them back and walked away because they stunk so bad.

The Deviled Egg Dribbles

Last week was Easter Sunday, and my grandparents came over to eat dinner with us. Now, I fart just about every second of the day, and my parents are mostly okay with it, but there is one single time that it is absolutely forbidden to fart. At the dinner table. My parents have told me more than enough times that farting at the dinner table is the worst, most terribly repulsive thing to do on this planet Earth.

To them, it'd probably be less disgusting to drink a gallon of milk that had been sitting outside for three weeks (gross right?!?!?). While I completely disagree with this, my parents are the lawmakers in the house, so it is something I don't do anymore. Because of this, you can probably assume that farting at the Easter dinner table would be something similar to a suicide attempt.

However, having my grandparents there with us gave me a free pass to do so and avoid the consequences of my actions.

My mom did the majority of the cooking for our big meal, and her food always brings out my gassiest self. Not only that, but she made deviled eggs in the spirit of the egg-themed holiday. It was a recipe for a gas-blaster disaster. Sitting at the dinner table I lost almost every ounce of my usual dinner time control and it completely stressed me out. On one of the few days where it is one hundred percent necessary to keep in all the emissions, I was unable to.

I had to do something about the planet-sized bomb in my bottom that would come out on its own if I kept ignoring it. After a failed attempt at asking to be excused, I knew I had to think quickly. Trusting my instincts, I let it go silently, and boy was it a doozy! To my luck, I was sitting right in between my grandparents, so when the stench hit everyone's noses, I quickly wrinkled my nose at both of them, in an attempt to make it look like I didn't know which one of them did it.

My mom wasn't fooled at first, but after I returned her death glare with a questioning shrug, she let me off the hook. She must have known that old people are prone to farting without knowing it. I mean, they don't use the term "old farts" for no reason. It took a good five minutes for the air to clear up around us, during which, neither my grandma or grandpa even noticed the smell, which worked really well in my favor. And that, my friends, is just one more reason why grandparents are the coolest.

Cute Farts

Farts are something that never really make me mad. I'm pretty accepting of all of the different kinds, as we all have better farting days than others. I'm definitely not the kind of person that judges my friends for not being able to fart as well as I can. However, there is one kind of fart that really just makes me want to scream every time that I hear them, and those are the farts that my sister and her friends do. They are so disgustingly cute and tiny and I just cannot stand them.

They sound like little squealing kittens (which is NOT how any fart should sound), and the worst part is that they act surprised and laugh when they do them! They should be embarrassed to fart like that because of how weak and annoyingly cute they sound! There had to be a way to get them to stop farting like that, so after thinking about for a little bit, I decided to go in my sister's room and teach them how.

I had already tried to teach my sister how to fart the right way, which didn't work very well, but I figured with her friend there, I might have a chance. After all, her friend Jill was kinda cute, and she might just appreciate me a little more if I taught her this useful skill. So, after I beat level 94 of BattleButts on my Bbox, I marched over to my sister's bedroom to teach her and Jill a lesson on bettering their boom bombs. They didn't notice me walk in the door, which I thought would be okay.

My plan was to do a really good fart, so good that they would have to turn around and see who did it, and maybe when Jill would see that it was me, she'd run up and kiss me and hug me and thank me for introducing her to the wonderful world of bottom blasts. Maybe she'd even come and play BattleButts with me! The excitement of my fantasy got the best of me, however, and before I knew it, I had already let my gas go.

I wasn't disappointed with the fart itself, because it was actually a pretty solid, hearty burst with an equally solid and hearty stench to it.

But, the reaction of the two girls was definitely not what I had anticipated. As soon as they had realized what I had done, their faces turned from happy to completely horrified. After seeing the look of disgust that my sister shot at me, I knew I had to run.

I bolted down the hall to my bedroom and locked the door behind me, my sister yelling back "MILO! DID YOU REALLY JUST COME INTO MY ROOM TO FART ON ME!?!?!?" The reaction I got was definitely not good, and I knew I'd probably get in trouble for it later. But, I didn't see what was the big deal. My sister and her friends always burp like truck drivers when they're together, so why was an alarming fart so horrifying? I guess I'll never understand girls.

Farts and Hugs

"Don't hug me too much," I often tell my mom. I come from a very "huggy" family. My parents have six and eight siblings, and those siblings have kids and even some grandchildren (So….way too many people to see!!!). As a result, we are obligated to go to a buttload of family reunions and random "congratulations!" celebrations on both sides of the family throughout the year.

Since we've moved to Flatula Flats, far away from the rest of the family, my parents feel even more like they have to return our old hometown a lot more often. While I know that there are lots of people who would love to have a ton of relatives like this to see and hang out with during the year, I'm more of a "hanging out by myself in my room eating pickle-flavored potato chips" kinda guy.

Family parties are just NOT my style. I think I'd like them better if I wasn't haunted by the childhood memory of Aunt Sheila coming over 3 times a week with a lukewarm green bean casserole for my family to eat for dinner, but I guess we'll never really know the true reason why.

My great aunt Shonda was turning 70 and we had to make the trip back to our hometown. Every dumb little thing that can be celebrated in my family (birthdays, weddings, baby showers, you name it) was celebrated with an annoyingly big party. This time the party was a picnic with barbecue (Pretty casual, might I add).

I knew there would be trouble, though, when I saw my Uncle Steve, crossfire coach and fitness extraordinaire. He is a big guy. And I mean BIG. His biceps are the size of watermelons and he has a sixteen pack of abs. He saw me and gave me the ultimate tight squeeze bear hug, and when you're just a kid like me, Uncle Steve is guaranteed to lift you right off of the ground while doing so. He might not know his own strength, too, because any little squeeze he gives make you feel like you stop breathing for a few seconds.

I don't really love these hugs, but what's worse is that there's always a pretty good chance that Steve is going to squeeze so hard that gas escapes my butt. It used to be kind of a joke when I was eight or nine years old but now I'm 10 and its not funny anymore. Not only do I like to be in control of my farts, but I guess once you reach a certain age (10 in my case), old middle aged dads just think you're being inappropriate.

I tried to and tried to defend myself and prove that my smelly little slip up was all Uncle Steve's fault, but none of the others believed me. it was so embarrassing! After that, the only people who would talk to me at the party were the really young and equally stinky little kids, and my grandparents who wanted to know what my favorite school subject was.

It was the worst family party ever, and I had thought that the parties themselves were terrible enough.

The Fart Summoner

At this point, you know that my farting abilities are far better than even the most gifted bottom blaster you may have met. I'll admit, I am a little bit self-obsessed, but I guarantee that you would be too if you had my amazing talents. I have gained so much control and fart wisdom, that you could call it a superpower by now. I know that I could even fight crime with my pepper spray squirts and laser-sharp spats.

Some days I even wonder if I could somehow use my farts like a jet pack, defying the laws of gravity (and the human body) by skyrocketing me towards space powered by my own man-made, pungent rocket fuel. With more training and research, I could even become a fart ninja and squeeze out some deadly, nasty clouds of gas powerful enough to blind bad guys. Wouldn't that be cool? I totally think so.

Now that it's summer break and I have more time to do things, I've decided to start researching ways that I can change the world one fart at a time.

I've heard stories of people using their farts like boat engines, tooting their way through the water without oars or any means of power other than their own bottoms. There are endless possibilities to what I could do with my lethal emissions. This is what I was put on the planet to do, I just know it.

So, by next school year, Milo Snotrocket is gonna be back and better than ever, as the master of the art of the fart, superfarterhero extraordinaire, and the very first Fart Ninja.

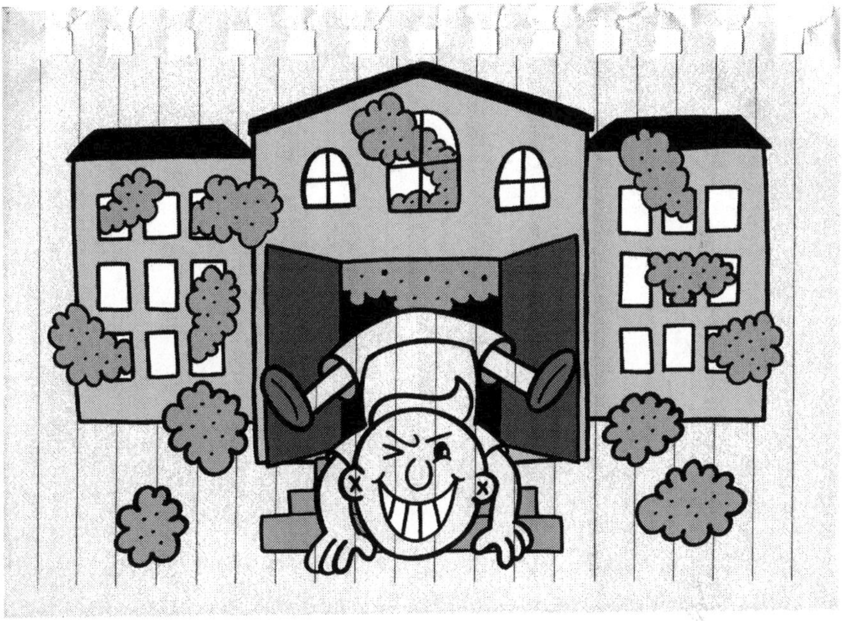

More Books by J.B. O'Neil

Hi Gang! I hope you liked "Santa Farts." Here are some more funny, cool books I've written that I think you'll like too...

http://jjsnip.com/fart-book

http://jjsnip.com/booger-fart-books

http://jjsnip.com/ninja-farts-book

http://jjsnip.com/caveman-farts

http://jjsnip.com/dog-farts

A long time ago, in a galaxy fart, fart away...

http://jjsnip.com/fart-wars

44

It's a turd, it's a sewer, no! It's...

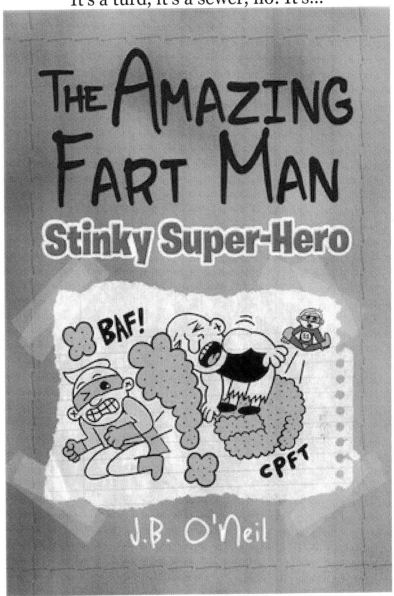

http://jjsnip.com/fartman

http://jjsnip.com/fart-ball

http://jjsnip.com/monster-farts

62063183R00031

Made in the USA
Middletown, DE
17 January 2018